Once upon a time saints

ethel Pochocki
with illustrations by tom matt

BETHLEHEM BOOKS · IGNATIUS PRESS

BATHGATE   SAN FRANCISCO

Revised Edition

First Printing, May 1996

ISBN 978-1-883937-15-7
Library of Congress: 96-83473

Cover design by Davin Carlson
Illustrations and cover art by Tom Matt

10194 Garfield St. S.
Bathgate, ND 58216
www.bethlehembooks.com
1-800-757-6831

Printed in the United States of America on acid free paper
Manufactured by Thomson-Shore, Dexter, MI (USA); RMA571LS636, January, 2011

Contents

*F*OR PARENTS, GRANDPARENTS,
GODPARENTS, SISTERS, BROTHERS, UNCLES, OR AUNTS
WHO FOR SOME REASON
FIND THIS BOOK IN YOUR HANDS

These stories were written to disarm rather than alarm. They are meant to show that the saints were not marshmallows—pale, sticky-sweet glops of goo that could be interesting only when toasted. They are meant to show human and lovable (most of the time) people whose passion for God led them into preposterous escapades.

Their lives are as unbelievable, as fantastic, as fairy tales of princesses with golden hair, princes on white stallions, blacker-than-hell witches, elves, pookahs, black ravens, white rabbits and smoke-belching dragons.

Fairy tales clear the way for sanctity. They are the child's first morality play, clear-cut, no-nonsense black and white, good and evil, life and death—with a bit of fun thrown in to alleviate the pain. The lives of the saints, so filled with derring-do, gaiety, charm and courage, are all the more fantastic because the persons were real, even though they might seem right out of the pages of Hans Christian Andersen.

You will not find dates and statistics here, except where they seem necessary to explain how or why a saint got to his particular spot. And I have used the embroidery of legend because I feel that under its eye-catching trivia, there is the good homespun of fact. Sometimes it has been hard to discover which facts are the *real* facts. In reading six books about one saint, you may have as many versions of his or her death—he may have died on the battlefield, in the arms of a wife or son, pinned to a tree with seven arrows . . . or a combination of all three.

I have chosen lesser-known saints because these are the ones to whom I am drawn, coaxing these hideaway saints out of the dusty pages of old reference books for one brief, if fanciful, moment in the sun.

Foreword

When you see a statue of a saint in church or a painting in a museum looking very long-faced and sour, please don't think saints were that way when they lived on earth. Most of them were very much like us. They laughed and cried and enjoyed picnics and ice cream and hopscotch, told jokes and had quick tempers. They probably pinched their baby brothers and were spanked for it when they were little. They might even have stolen apples from the store and lied about it. Certainly they hid their liver under their plates at suppertime.

But then something happened. God spoke to them, and they stopped what they were doing and listened, and every thing was different from then on. They took their ordinary lives and made them into *extra*ordinary adventures.

No matter who they were (farmers or soldiers or queens or jugglers), they knew where they were going. They made butter, washed lepers, sailed to Nova Scotia, taught children the alphabet, or whatever God gave them to do, as perfectly as possible. They knew that God was always with them so nothing could frighten them—not even thunderstorms, spiders or death.

They loved this world as well as Heaven. The birds and beasts and everything God had made were their friends. They tried to see Christ in all people, even those who were a pain, a bore, or just plain nasty. It wasn't easy, but they knew God loved them, so they tried.

The saints teach us one important thing—that we don't have to follow anyone else's way to holiness. All we have to do is want to be saints, in our own way and using our special gifts, and God will send that gift of grace with each sunrise. That grace will help you master the bumps in the day ahead.

If you want to be a saint badly (or goodly) enough, then you will, and someone a few hundred years from now may be writing a story about *you!*

$\mathcal{A}$lice

Once upon a time in the country of Burgundy, there lived a princess named Alice. When she was two years old, her father, King Rudolf, said to King Hugh of Italy, "Hugh, I think your son, Lothair, is a handsome, smart fellow. He should be just right for my daughter in about fourteen years. What do you say to an engagement?"

Hugh thought that was a fine idea, so the two kings signed a paper saying that Alice and Lothair were to be wed. Everyone celebrated at a great feast, with Sparkling Burgundy for the grown-ups and raspberry ice-cream for the children.

When Alice was sixteen, she became queen of Italy. She would have been very happy except for Lothair's brother, Berengarius. He was as dark and evil as Lothair was bright and good. He was very jealous of his brother and his bride, for he wanted the throne for himself.

The young couple ruled Italy justly and kindly for three years, and then Lothair died. (Some say his brother poisoned him.) Berengarius tried to persuade Alice to marry his son. When she refused (she didn't even like his son), the angry brother imprisoned her in his castle on Lake Garda.

Alice felt as if the world had come to an end. After years of being

1

loved and treated royally, here she was in a bleak castle dungeon, in a rough itchy dress that didn't fit, and her beautiful hair no longer hung with ribbons and jewels but cut blunt and uneven. She was glad she had no mirror to see it. "This is no way for a queen to be treated," she sniffled. She was alone, abandoned, friendless. It even hurt to cry, because her nose was already red and sore from a cold brought on by the dampness.

Then God spoke to her, quietly so as not to startle her. "Be of good heart, Alice. Don't you know I will rescue you at just the right moment? Dry your eyes and open your ears—*listen*."

All Alice could hear was the scurrying of hard-shelled black bugs, up and down the walls, to and fro, hither and thither, across the floor and under the door. But above this came the sound of tap-tap-tapping. It came from the grate of the window set high above her.

She stepped carefully over the bugs and looked up to see an old priest who had been her friend when she lived in the palace. He had not forgotten his Queen and had come with a plan to rescue her. First, he would dig a tunnel from outside where he was, to under the cell where she was. Then he would come up under one of the stones on the floor, which Alice would have to loosen.

It sounded impossible to Alice, but she remembered that nothing was impossible if God was helping. She prayed that the priest wouldn't get caught and that the black bugs wouldn't eat her toes while she was waiting. In a few days there was a thumping and knocking under the very stone she was kneeling on. She pried it loose, and there was the face of her friend, the priest. "Come quickly," he whispered, "follow me, and pull the stone down after you." She did as she was told, just as the guard came to see about those strange noises in the Queen's cell. The stone moved slightly, and his eye caught it.

"Oh no, you don't! Come back here this moment, Your Majesty, you're not allowed to escape! Excuse me, Your Majesty, but you better watch out because I'm coming down after you!"

And he jumped down the hole after them. But they had scrambled through the tunnel so easily, they were through and out in no time flat. The priest bid Alice goodbye, for he had to be back to his rectory for dinner so his housekeeper wouldn't suspect anything. Alice thanked him and began to make her way through the dark, unfamiliar wood.

Suddenly she began sinking in the mud. It came up to her ankles, then her knees, and she felt as if she were stuck in a glob of cold, thick molasses. When it got to her waist, she cried out to her guardian angel to get her out of this mess.

The sound of galloping horses drew nearer and nearer, and just as the mud reached Alice's armpits, a band of soldiers in strange uniforms appeared. The leader jumped off his horse and, standing on the firm, rocky soil, he reached over and pulled her to safety.

He told Alice he was Otto, the Emperor of Germany, and he had come to Italy to defeat the evil Berengarius. "Good!" said Alice.

When he accomplished this, Alice no longer had to hide. She was free. Otto, who had fallen in love with her when he first saw her in the mud, asked her to marry him and to become the Empress of Germany. Alice thought this would be lovely, for she had fallen in love with *him* when he pulled her out of the mud, and so they were wed on Christmas Day.

The German people loved Alice and called her "a marvel of grace and beauty." She was indeed a marvel, for in her lifetime she would be princess, queen, empress, wife, and (after Otto died) nun.

Everything that happened in her life, Alice handled with grace. Nevertheless, she still would shudder whenever she heard the sound of those black, hard-shelled bugs scurrying around in the dark.*

* Alice is also known as Adelaide or Adelheid.

Ambrose

Once upon a time, there was a saint named Ambrose whose words were so sweet, they were "good as honey from a comb." As a matter of fact, when he was a very small baby, sleeping outside in his carriage in the palace courtyard, a swarm of bees did alight on him and pay him a visit.

They covered his face and mouth and walked up and down his nose and in and out his ears. His mother gasped when she saw them and was about to wave them away when Ambrose's father stopped her.

"Let them be, my dear," he said, "they will surely sting him if we upset them. If we are very quiet, they should take their leave soon."

And within minutes they did take off in a big buzzing bunch and soared out of sight. The father, who was a respected governor of northern Italy, felt that this unusual happening was an omen that Ambrose would someday be very important. Perhaps he might be a governor, just like his father! What could give his parents more pride or pleasure than that?

Ambrose grew up and studied hard and became a lawyer and judge. His father had died, and Ambrose knew that he was probably telling everyone in Heaven about his talented son. Probus, the Prefect of Rome (the Head Governor of all the governors in the Roman Empire), felt that

Ambrose was smart and wise enough to be the governor of Milan, so he sent him off there with a pat on the back and a pocketful of gold and pencils. "Go and act as a bishop, not as a judge," he said jokingly.

The people in Milan were quick to see that Ambrose ruled with fairness and good sense and they loved him for this. He was so good at settling disagreements, his office was always filled with angry neighbors muttering or punching or pulling each other's hair. But whatever he decided, they accepted without a grumble. His word was the law. They knew he would give the perfect, just answers to their problems.

At that time, there were those who called themselves Arians—Christians who did not believe that Christ was really God. There were a good many of them, among them the most wealthy and respectable citizens of the country. Even the Empress Justina was one. Ambrose tried to keep peace between the two kinds of Christians because he was governor of all the people.

One day, an Arian bishop died suddenly, and a fight began to brew. There was to be an election for a new bishop and both sides wanted their choices to win. Ambrose went to the election and tried to calm down the shouting crowd. For a moment it became very quiet, and then from the mob came a child's voice, sharp and clear: "Ambrose for Bishop."

The crowd, in agreement for once, yelled, "Yes, yes! We want *Ambrose!*" But he laughed at such foolishness. First of all, he said, he wasn't even baptized, although he considered himself a Christian in his heart. And furthermore, he wasn't a priest, so how could he be a bishop?

The people paid no attention and yelled louder, "Ambrose for Bishop!" He began to get worried. He went home, and the crowd followed him and banged on the gates to his palace.

Ambrose decided to run away to a friend's home until he could figure out what to do. He left by a secret side door in the dark of the night. He could barely see the road and took a wrong turn. Unknown to him, he traveled all night in circles. When dawn came, he found that he had come right back to his palace, where the people were still waiting for him.

They surrounded him and vowed they would not let him go until he promised to become their bishop. He sent word to Probus the Prefect to please help him, but Probus replied with delight that he thought Ambrose would make a *perfect* bishop and he was pleased that his governor was so highly thought of by the people!

Ambrose saw that this must be God's will for him and there was no way he could avoid it. Within seven days, he was baptized, ordained a priest, and pronounced Bishop of Milan. He gave away everything he owned to the poor and his land to the church and sold many of the gold and silver ornaments in the church to buy food and wood and wool stockings for the cold and hungry.

Some people sniffed at this, saying it was a shame the way the new bishop didn't appreciate beauty and that he had no right to treat God's property so shabbily.

"Which do you think more important," Ambrose asked quietly, "the ornaments which hang in cold and lifeless beauty, or living people with souls?" He called the money he gave to the poor "the gold of Christ that saves men from death."

The Empress Justina, who had not wanted Ambrose to be Bishop, decided to take one of his churches to use as an Arian temple. She felt that because she was an Empress, she could take what she wanted.

But Ambrose shook his head and said, "Sorry, Your Majesty. Palaces are matters for the Empress, but churches belong to the Bishop. And since what you want is not right, I can't let you have a church."

Justina was furious. She would show that little pip-squeak of a bishop just who was in charge! (Ambrose, a small man with a cloud of pale yellow hair like a dandelion, was used to being called a pipsqueak.) She ordered her soldiers to take over the largest cathedral, where Ambrose usually preached, on Palm Sunday.

Ambrose, knowing what she was about, preached the sermon that day on holding fast and not giving up one's faith—or church—because of fear. He told the congregation of Justina's plan and of the soldiers even at that moment surrounding the cathedral.

They whispered among themselves and then began quietly cheer-

ing. "We stay with you, Ambrose. No one shall leave or enter this holy place!"

To pass the time, Ambrose taught them hymns which he had composed during nights when he didn't sleep. After they had learned the chants and simple melodies, Ambrose said, "Now let's do it in harmony!"

He gave the ladies and the men and the children each a different part to sing and when they put it all together, the music soared to the ceiling and out the windows like curling wisps of incense. It was so sweet even the bees in the flowers on the altar stopped buzzing to listen.

They sang this day and the next and the next, and when they had sung everything they knew, Ambrose would pull out another psalm or proverb he had set to music, and they would start in all over again.

On Good Friday, the Empress gave in. She did not change her mind, but she knew when she could not win. The country's sympathy was with Ambrose and his flock of singers, and even her soldiers outside the church had begun to hum the hymns and pass them along to their friends. Why, the Empress, herself, sang them aloud to herself, alone in her room. (Or so it was told by the maid who made the beds in the royal chamber.)

For many years, twenty-three to be exact, Ambrose governed as a well-loved bishop. His door was always open each day for anyone who wanted advice, and while his candle burned through the night hours, he wrote his books and letters and hymns.

His words, written or spoken, were sweet, simple and wise. They healed and soothed like a teaspoonful of honey. You may have had a dessert called Ambrosia—oranges and apples and coconut and honey served cold on a hot day in a pretty crystal bowl.

Like Ambrose, it is sweet, refreshing, and simply Heavenly!

$\mathcal{A}$nne

Once upon a time there was a grandmother named Anne who was special. Now, I know all grandmothers are special, especially yours and mine. They are like that extra gift under the Christmas tree you didn't expect. Grandmothers let you sleep in their big brass beds on cold starched sheets under piles of feather quilts, and they make blueberry pancakes for you the next morning. They have time to sit and rock and say nothing at all while you pat their hair or arms, and they love the little bunches of dandelions you bring them. They let you peel apples for pie and hang sheets on the line and pretend they are sails for pirate ships. They are a lot like mothers, only they don't scold as much.

Anne was even more special because she was Jesus' grandmother. She never expected to be a grandmother. She never even thought she would be a mother. She and her husband, Joachim, had prayed and waited, and waited and prayed for years that God would send them a child. As the years passed, Anne grew older and tried not to feel hurt that God had not heard her prayer.

"If that is how God wants it," she sighed, "then I must accept it—but I can't understand why."

She tried to cover up her sadness by becoming everyone's favorite

aunt. She made large round sugar cookies for all the children of the neighborhood and washed the blood off their scraped knees and sewed the rips in their torn robes when their mothers were too busy.

One day when Joachim had gone out to the desert to fast and pray, Anne was sitting by a laurel bush when an angel appeared to her and said, "Anne, the Lord has heard your prayer and you shall conceive and bear a child, and your seed shall be spoken of in all the world!"

And Anne believed the angel and was overjoyed. She promised that whether it be a boy or girl, she would bring it as a gift to the Lord. At the same time, an angel also appeared to Joachim, who had been praying in the desert, relaying the same news. At first Joachim was frightened. He thought he had been out too long in the sun. But when he came home and Anne greeted him with this exciting news, he too believed that God had finally heard their prayers, and he and his wife hugged each other with happiness.

When a daughter was born to them, they called her Mary. Anne remembered her promise. As soon as Mary could toddle, Anne took her to the temple and told the priests about her and they said that she would bring great joy not only to her parents but also the whole world.

Little else is known about Anne, except that God must have thought her the one perfect person to be Mary's mother and Jesus' grandmother. She is the patron saint of all grandmothers, without whom life wouldn't be half as much fun. Can you imagine all the kisses the world would lose if there weren't grandmothers?

Perhaps you never got to meet your grandmother, but you will someday. She is probably, right now, talking with Anne in heaven about the party they will have when you join them.

Barbara

Once upon a time, in the town of Heliopolis in Egypt, there lived a bright and charming girl called Barbara. She was the only child of Dioscorus, one of the town's leading citizens. They lived a very comfortable life in a large, beautiful home with many windows and balconies. It sat high up on a slope where they could look out over the town as they ate supper on the sunporch.

Barbara had almost everything she wanted—but not quite. She did not have a mother. Her mother had died when Barbara was born, and she missed having one to hug her and brush her hair and talk to as they walked in the garden. Her father tried to make up for this by giving her all his attention and love, except that it wasn't a real love.

He didn't want to share her with anyone and made sure she never left the house. She couldn't visit a friend or sleep overnight or play games or go swimming. She didn't know what life was like outside her home.

By the time she was twenty years old, she was a strange mixture of a girl. She could solve geometry problems and read fables in Greek without blinking an eye. But she knew nothing of what went on in the world. She saw no one other than her father, the servants, and a frightened little man who was her tutor.

He was the one who told her a little of the exciting world outside—which to her was the marketplace in town. He would bring her little gifts—a peacock feather, a pomegranate, and, once, a real white rabbit with pink eyes. And when he felt that he had taught her everything he knew and was about to leave, he brought her one final present.

"But," he whispered, making sure no one was listening, "first you must promise me that you will never, never let anyone see it or know who gave it to you, *especially* your father!"

Barbara laughed because the poor man was shaking and she thought that silly. "Of course I won't," she said kindly, "but you must know my father loves me and would never harm me or my friends, if I had any."

The tutor took a small book from beneath his coat. "Please read this," he said. "It has changed my life and perhaps it will yours too."

He bowed, kissed her hand, and left quickly. Barbara opened the book with curiosity. It was called **THE NEW TESTAMENT.** As Barbara began to read, she saw it was about those Christians whom her father hated so bitterly. He hated them more than taxes, black flies, lukewarm coffee, or little boys who stole figs from his trees at night.

Barbara had heard about these people who said the love of God and their neighbors was the most important thing in life. Why did her father hate them so?

Page after page, the words filled her heart and found a home there.

17

She wanted to know more about Christ so she wrote a letter to a man called Origen of Alexandria, who had writings about this book, and sent it to him secretly by an old servant whom she trusted.

A few weeks later, Barbara was on her knees working in her egg-plant garden, thinking about Our Lord's stories of seeds and vines and fruit, when she noticed a new gardener raking about the rose bushes. Now who was he, she wondered. She had not seen him before. He raked closer to her and whispered, "Young lady, Origen sent me. Can we go somewhere? I have much to share with you."

They went off to the old summer house and the gardener disclosed that he was really a Christian priest sent to teach her about the new faith, and even baptize her if she wished. "Oh yes, right now, don't waste a moment!" Barbara agreed excitedly. After he baptised her, she breathed a great sigh of satisfaction. Now she could give her life completely to following Christ. The priest left quietly, and not a moment too soon, for Barbara's father appeared, frowning, wondering "Now who is that gardener and where did he take off to? When did I hire him?"

Barbara wasn't listening. She was so happy, she glowed. Her father smiled at her and was certain he had done the right thing in keeping his daughter to himself. If she were not happy, would her eyes sparkle and dance as they did? Barbara yearned to share her new life with her father, but she remembered the tutor and kept quiet.

The next day, Dioscorus left to go on a business trip. He gave Barbara the task of seeing to it that two new windows were put into a bathroom. She brought her crocheting outside and supervised the carpenters and bricklayers doing the job. As the windows were being fitted into place, she had an idea.

"As long as you are putting in two windows, would you please add another, right next to the others? It will be all right, my father won't mind," she assured them. And so they did.

When her father returned and saw what had been done, he screwed his eyebrows into a frown and bellowed, "What is this? Three windows when I specifically told you two?"

"It's my doing, Father, I told them to do it," said Barbara, a bit fearful but still excited by the idea of sharing her faith with him. "I had a reason. I wanted you to see that true light enters the soul through the Father, the Son, and the Holy Spirit. The Christian God is all three of these in one person. I know, because I am now a Christian!"

Dioscorus went into a purple rage. His precious, lovely daughter—one of those ugly, hateful Christians! He let out a terrible roar and chased her up the marble staircase until she reached her room and bolted the door. Her father stopped screaming and asked, in a quiet, sly voice, if she would go for a walk with him so they could talk further about this matter.

She unbolted the door, happy that her father had come around, and they walked arm-in-arm out of the house. Her father opened the gate to the woods beyond, and they climbed through cedar groves to the top of the hill. Here Dioscorus, still angered because she vowed to be a Christian forever, unsheathed his sword and killed her on the spot.

The sky grew dark and thunder growled and lightning bolts chased her father as he ran sobbing down the hill. One streak flashed brilliant red, and Dioscorus fell on his sword, dead.

Barbara barely had a chance to follow Christ in her life. She could not offer Our Lord a list of Good Deeds or Offerings-Up. She had time only to be steadfast. She knew what she had to do and she did it. It was as simple and brave as that.

The next time the skies crackle and rumble during a thunderstorm, don't hide under the bed or pull the sheet over your head. Ask Barbara for the courage to look it right in the eye.

Barnaby of Compiegne

Once upon a time in France, there lived a juggler named Barnaby. At that time, a juggler was a street-person, a show by himself. He would wander through the towns and, seeing a good-sized crowd at a fair or marketplace, he would lay down a little carpet, get out his copper balls or plates or knives, and set to work to entertain the crowd.

Sometimes jugglers dressed like clowns, with bells on their caps and toes and with special costumes, so that each juggler was known by his colors and silks. Barnaby's were blue and white because he had a deep love for our Lady and this was his way of honoring her. When he tossed the balls and knives so perfectly up and around and down, never missing one, and when he tumbled and rolled himself up into a circle and the people clapped and clapped, he thanked Mary in his heart for giving him his one and only talent.

Barnaby loved juggling. It was what he did best. But when it rained, he had no audience and no way to eat. People threw pennies, carrots, roses—whatever they had with them—to show their appreciation of his art, and that is how he lived. But when it rained. . . .

One of those miserable rainy days Barnaby was sitting by the road, wondering where to go, when a monk from a nearby monastery happened by. He had heard of Barnaby, the juggler in the blue and white silk, so he stopped to ask him how he was, and, by the way, why did he dress that way? Barnaby explained, and the monk was so impressed he said, "Well, if you love Mary so much, you should be in a monastery praising her and doing worthwhile things, like painting or making statues or writing poems to her. You shouldn't be wasting your life out on the streets, throwing balls in the air for money!"

Barnaby thought it would be wonderful to live in a monastery, and he went with the monk, who was the prior, that very day. At first he was very happy. He did all the work he was given and then he was free to go to the chapel to talk to Mary. One of the monks had carved a beautiful statue from white marble of Mary holding her baby, Jesus, and Barnaby would look into her eyes and talk to her, telling her how he wished he could do something beautiful for her as the other monks did.

One day an idea came to him which excited him inside. He told no one for fear he would be laughed at, or even that he might be forbidden to do such a strange thing. Every evening after supper, Barnaby disappeared for a while and went to the chapel. This went on for weeks. The prior grew curious as to what the little monk was doing there, so he and another monk quietly followed Barnaby in the shadows of the hallway. Who knew what this crazy fellow might be doing? After all, Barnaby had been just a juggler before he came to the monastery to live.

23

The two monks got to the chapel and peered through the tiny window. Their mouths dropped open with shock. There, before the altar, Barnaby was performing every trick he had ever known, juggling his copper balls in a rhythm so skillful it seemed like a never-ending wheel of motion. The monks looked at each other, their shock turning to anger. How dare Barnaby act this way in front of the Mother of God? Had he no respect? Acting like a common street performer, jumping, dancing, yes, even sweating!

The prior was about to rush in and grab the juggler, who he thought must be mad, and hurry him out of the chapel, when he saw Barnaby fall to the floor in exhaustion.

The prior could not budge. He saw the marble statue of Mary move down from the altar and come over to Barnaby. She bent down and wiped the sweat from his brow and said, "Thank you, my dear son. It has been a long time since Jesus and I have seen such beautiful juggling. We could watch you every day and not get tired. But *you* are tired and you must rest. Go, now." Then she moved slowly back to the altar.

The two monks left the chapel window without a word to each other. They knew without speaking that this was to be Barnaby's secret between him and his Lady and they would not spoil it for him. They knew that Barnaby's gift of himself was as important to Mary as any work of art the other monks created.

Benedict of San Fradello

Once upon a time in the sunny land of Sicily, there lived a slave named Benedict. He was black and even in those days it was not easy to be black. People made fun of his colour, his parents, his clothes, the way his hair curled tight, but Benedict trained himself not to listen, and, more importantly, not to let it hurt him. God had spoken to him, so for God's sake, he could answer calmly and with love, or else not at all.

One day a well-known nobleman named Lanzi passed by while the usual making-fun-of-Benedict was going on. He was so impressed with Benedict's patience and gentleness, he had him set free. Lanzi asked Benedict if he would like to join a group of friends and himself and retire to a life of prayer.

Everything inside Benedict said, "Yes!" And he accepted with gladness. After many years, the nobleman died, and Benedict, who had become so admired for his quiet, wise ways, was named superior. He accepted, although he would rather have stayed in the kitchen where he felt at home and where he produced as many miracles as loaves of bread.

Like many saints, Benedict had the gift of multiplying bread, especially when it was needed to feed the poor. Each day he gave away every bit of bread stored in the pantry only to find the shelves filled with more

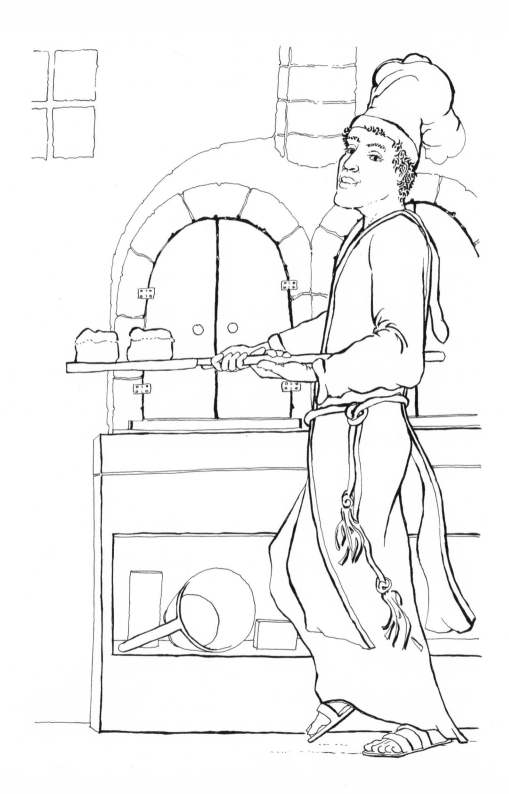

than in the beginning. Benedict had a very special feeling for bread, remembering how Jesus had turned it into his body at the Last Supper, and he would not let one crust be wasted.

When the monks scraped the plates, he made sure that any pieces of bread were saved for the poor or the birds. Sometimes the monks joked about Benedict's being so serious over "garbage."

"This food is the blood of those who have given it to us for the love of God," he would say and try to look stern.

One day the monks' smiles froze on their faces when Benedict, finding some bread crusts floating in the dishwater, pulled a cleaning brush from the water and squeezed blood from it. From that time on, the monks wasted not one crumb.

His fame as a wise counselor spread so that the sick, the learned, the beggar, the archbishop, all came to ask advice of the black monk in the kitchen. He became the patron saint of people with headaches and, I would imagine, dishwashers.

The next time you burn your toast and want to throw it in the garbage, think of Benedict. It might not be as hopeless as you think and perhaps you could save it with a bit of raspberry jam. If it is really burnt, so that the whole kitchen is filled with smoke, think of the birds. Remember that bread is one of God's special gifts.

Christopher

Once upon a time, in the land of Canaan, there lived a giant named Offero. He wasn't just a very big man who ate too many banana splits and french fries, he was a *real giant*. He was even bigger than the Philistine giant that David slew with his slingshot.

It is told that Offero was twelve cubits in length (which is about twenty-four feet) and that he "was of a right great stature and had a terrible and fearful face and appearance." Some said that with his shaggy, uncombed hair, which covered small piercing eyes, he looked like a very mean dog. Since he had a rude and rough way about him, no one ever said this to his face. No one liked the idea of being squashed by a giant hand.

Because of his size, Offero was bound to stick out like a (large) sore thumb. But he rather enjoyed it. He was the village strong man, and did odd jobs such as pulling up trees that were in the way of traffic, moving a herd of camels, chopping down a forest, and all sorts of things. He was very handy to have around.

Even though you couldn't see what was going on in Offero's brain under all that hair, it was working continually. He knew what great strength he had and felt that he could do more with it than stay in his home village and putter around. He decided that he would search for the most powerful king in the world. He would find this perfect master and serve him. So he packed a few barrels of food in his knapsack and started off. His friends were sorry to see him go, as you can imagine. Who would they get now to move those granite slabs even three men couldn't budge but Offero could lift without popping a muscle?

He traveled for four months, until he came to a town that was in the midst of a great festival. When he asked what it was all about, the people told him that the most powerful king in the world was coming to open their yearly games. So Offero sought him out and knelt before him, and everyone scurried away because of the dust he raised.

"Oh, Your Majesty," he said, "I hear you are the most powerful king in the world and because I am the strongest man, I would like to serve you. We could do wonders together."

The king was astonished. No one could have given him a more valuable gift than all this strength. He gave Offero the title of King's Official Strong Man and soon had him busy building moats and putting flagpoles on top of castles. Offero became part of the court, and the poor cook had to prepare two banquets a night, one for the king and his family and friends, and the other for Offero.

One night during an ordinary banquet, a minstrel came to the castle and asked if he might entertain them while they were eating. The king thought some dinner music would be quite nice so the minstrel took up his harp and began playing. He sang of brave and heroic and mysterious deeds.

Offero noticed that every time a certain name was sung, the king bowed his head and shook and crossed himself. Finally, being very curious, he asked the king why he did this. The king whispered, "I fear that name the Prince of Darkness, the King of Evil, *Satan!*" And he crossed himself again.

Offero was crushed. His king was not so mighty after all, for he feared this Satan. The giant knew he must leave. "I'm sorry, Your Majesty," he said, "but if Satan is more powerful than you, then I must find him and serve him." And Offero started off again on his journey to find the perfect master.

After three days of walking, he came upon a bunch of growling, scratching, spitting, dirty, shrieking men. In the midst of them, astride a menacing black horse, sat a dark figure, completely clad in black armor and helmet. The men looked at Offero and quieted down.

The giant came up to the black figure. "Are you Satan? I am seeking the most powerful ruler in the world? Are you he?"

Satan smiled. He had been waiting for him these three days. "Seek no further, Offero, I am the mightiest ruler of earth and sky and universe. Come and join me! I have need of no man, but you could be of use to me, if you like."

So Offero and Satan and the mewling, mauling, hideously laughing band of men set off together. After a small distance, they came to a cross-road, and at the point of turning right or left, a pilgrim had put up two tree limbs in the shape of a cross. The green wood was fastened together with bark. Satan stopped short and put his hand over his helmet. He bent over as though blinded and his horse shook and foamed at the mouth.

"Quickly," he charged the men, "go the other way so we don't have to see this accursed thing!"

Offero was greatly puzzled. The mightiest ruler of the universe, frightened of two pieces of wood? He stepped boldly up to Satan and asked him why he acted this way.

"Upon that cross the Son of God died so you foolish men could never again be my slaves. I hate it, for the truth of his Cross is more powerful than I!"

So Offero said, "Well then, I must leave you and find this God of whom you have such fear," and off he went once more.

"Where are you, God?" He looked behind every tree but found nothing. He picked up a boulder and to his surprise found an old man in a brown robe sitting there, enjoying the sun.

Offero asked the hermit, for that is what he was, if he knew where he might find God. "Of course," said the hermit, blinking in the sun.

"Where?" asked Offero, excitedly.

"First you must fast and pray," said the hermit.

"What do you mean? What is 'fast and pray'?" Offero frowned. There were so many things he did not understand.

The hermit with the wisdom of his years saw that Offero was not yet ready to do these things, so he said, "You can also find Christ in serving others. It is not easy, but it is a sure way. A few miles from here is a wild stream, filled with rushing rapids and whirlpools and deep holes. The only time it can be crossed is in the summer when it quiets down somewhat. It would save people many miles of walking around the river, if they could get across. My huge brother, will you be their ferryman and use your great body to help them across?"

Offero laughed. What a simple job! Surely this would be child's play; after all, was he not the strongest man in the world? He felt it was almost too easy a way to serve his new master.

He thanked the hermit and went to the river. He built a small hut on its bank where he might live; it was small for Offero but the hermit would have rattled around in it. All day long he carried people from one side of the river to the other, men riding horses, women carrying children and baskets of eggplants. He cut down a tree to use as a staff in steadying himself in the water. From being always in the sun and water, it became polished and hard.

Offero searched the faces of everyone he helped. Which one would

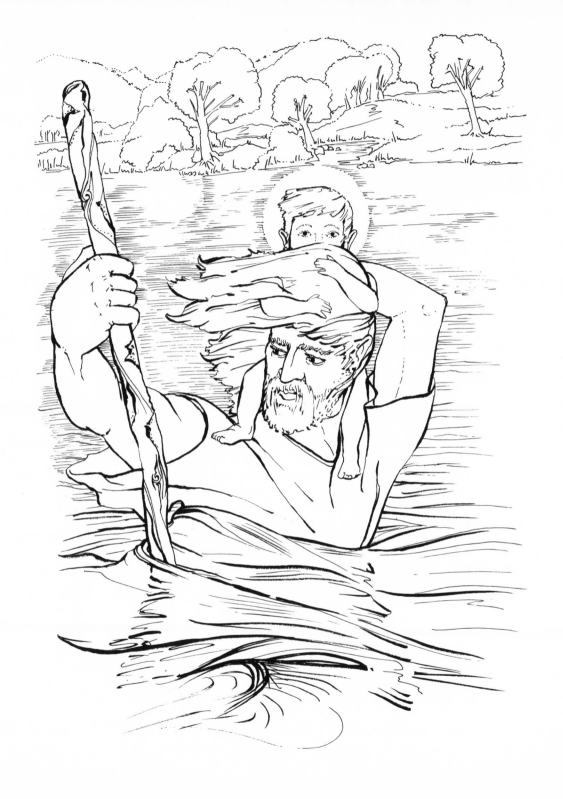

be Christ? Would he come along with his royal party, dressed in royal purple satin? He must remember to carry him very carefully so water would not stain his robes. Then Christ would be very impressed with Offero's ability and would say to him on the spot, "Come, Offero, I've been waiting for you. You need seek your perfect master no longer."

One evening at twilight, just before the stars came out and the birds were singing their evensong and the wind sighed as softly as doves in the morning, Offero heard a small voice and felt a tug at his leg.

"What is this? Some mosquito speaks to me?"

He looked down to brush it away and saw a very small child who looked up at him with sweet sad eyes. "Offero, Offero, will you carry me across the river tonight? I am alone and need your help."

Offero laughed with pleasure. This would be easy! "Of course, little one. We shall be over before you know it, climb up onto my shoulders. Why, you are so little, you can fit on one shoulder!"

He helped the child up and Offero started into the water with his featherweight load. Suddenly, the waves grew high and rough, the rapids swirled and rose under his feet, nearly toppling him. The child weighed more heavier and heavier upon his shoulder. For the first time in his life, Offero was afraid that he would not be able to carry his burden.

He barely made it to the other side, tottered feebly and begged the child to please jump off. The giant lay down on the shore and looked up at the child who was smiling at him and was bathed in a golden light.

"Dear Offero," he said, "you have carried the one whom you seek and all the cares and sins of the world which he has taken upon himself. How pleasing to me is your work! From now on you will not be called Offero, but 'Christofer,' the Christ-bearer."

Then the child vanished and Christopher (or Christofer, if you prefer) knelt down and kissed the spot where he had been. Christopher knew he had found his Perfect Master at last.

Christopher had a very special gift. He could not write poetry or split an atom or tap dance. All he could do was use his strength to help Christ carry the world and lighten his load. And he did!

He still does. Call on him when you need to move a mountain (or just take the trash out of the cellar or carry an unjust accusation in your heart). Your load will become as light as thistledown.

Clement

Once upon a time there was an early bishop of Rome (some say he came after Peter) named Clement. If you look up the word *clement* in the dictionary, you will find it means mild and merciful, and Clement was all that. Like Felix and Dorothy, he tried to witness his belief in Christ and outwit those who would kill him for it. Often there was no place to hide, and the Christians had to face the fact that they would most likely be caught. So Clement was not surprised when he was. But for some reason, the Emperor Trajan did not throw Clement to the lions or have him beheaded. Instead, Trajan banished Clement to the country of Crimea. The bishop knew he could never come back to Rome, but he realized that God must have work for him to do in this unknown land. Many of his friends went with him to show their love, and so Clement had company to work with him in the marble quarries of Crimea.

It was hard, hot, dusty work and they suffered because the supply of water ran out. If they had been Indians, perhaps they would have danced a prayer for rain, but instead they knelt and swayed and bowed as they asked God to please send cool, clear water to soothe their throats and quench their thirsts.

While they were praying, trying to think about God's grace coming down like rain, a small white lamb came out from under the puckerbrush and nuzzled Clement's arm. Clement had never seen the animal before, nor any lamb for that matter, so he knew that the lamb must have been sent by our Lord. He followed the animal who led him to a grassy spot nearby and pawed the ground until Clement understood. He took a shovel and pick and began spading with all his strength.

"Keep praying, friends!" he yelled back to his companions, and before two minutes passed, a stream of water gushed from the hole. Everyone ran to it and washed their faces and swallowed large gulps of the water and danced in their wet clothes. When Clement turned to thank the lamb, there was no sign of him, not in the puckerbrush, not anywhere, ever again.

Because of this, many of the other slaves began to believe in this Christ of whom Clement spoke. This so angered the Emperor, who thought he had gotten rid of this Christian bother, that he ordered the soldiers to tie an anchor around Clement and toss him into the sea, so no one would ever find him. His followers went searching for him and prayed God to direct them. As they stood on the shore, the sea went back three miles until Clement's body was found, in a marble shrine which the angels had built for him at the bottom of the sea.

Whenever you see a picture of Clement, you will see that he has an anchor around him. One church in England has an anchor instead of a rooster for a weather vane in Clement's honor. Perhaps that is why we call it "Clement" weather—when the weather is good.

Comgall

Once upon a time in the town of Bangor in Ireland, there lived a monk called Comgall. He was so well known as a teacher that all the parents who lived around the monastery sent their sons to study with him. The boys learned all the important things from Comgall, such as how to print a manuscript, play the harp and sing the psalms in Latin, but most of all they learned how to love and understand the wild birds and beasts and bugs. Comgall's special gift from God was to be accepted as brother by every living thing that crawled or flew or walked on four feet.

Once when they were walking past a pond, Comgall and his students saw six haughty swans, admiring themselves in the mirror of water. The boys called to the swans but the birds squawked and honked with great scorn. The idea of going to humans! Comgall smiled and told the boys to stay back and watch. Then he walked into the water a little way, called to the swans—and such a sight! Flapping and trumpeting, they surrounded him. One came close and would not be happy until Comgall petted him. But when the boys crept closer, eager to touch the swans, they all flew off.

Comgall could charm even the mice of the village, and once he did.

At this time, there was a famine in Ireland. Everybody was hungry, including Comgall and the monks and their pupils. Comgall knew where there was food to be had. Prince Croadh had barns full of oats and wheat and barley which could be made into porridges and bread and ale. But Croadh was a selfish man whose first thought was for himself, and whose second thought was for his mother. His mother, whose name was Luch, was just as mean and stingy as her son, only more so because she had had more years of practice at it.

Now *Luch* means mouse in Irish and that gave Comgall an idea of how he could get the miser to share his grain and also to teach him and his mother that God did not want him to hoard God's good gifts for himself alone while others needed them.

Comgall first asked Croadh if he would share his grain.

"You must be crazy!"

Would he sell it?

"Of course not!"

Would he trade it for a silver goblet which belonged to Comgall?

"Not on your life," Croadh laughed coldly. "You keep your cup and I keep my grain. Every bit of it for me and my Mouse!"

Comgall saw that the prince wouldn't budge, so he sighed and thought, "Very well, I have a mouse or two up my sleeve, too."

He went home and called his friends the mice together to discuss the situation. Each mouse offered his idea, was listened to, and given proper attention. Finally, they decided on a strategy. Then the mouse with the shortest tail carried the word throughout the mice colony of Bangor and all waited, alert for action.

That night every mouse of every age came out of his home and together they formed a long line which moved like a giant serpent up and down the road to Croadh's barn. Hundreds and thousands of mice crawled into the barn and ate one kernel apiece and carried one back with them. The younger ones ate more so they would have enough energy for the return trip. When they scurried out of the barn, there was not one stray, loose, neglected, stomped-on, hidden-under-a-bit-of-hay grain to be found.

Prince Croadh was furious when he discovered his empty barn. He sputtered and hopped and tore his hair. His mother hobbled out to see what the racket was about. Then *she* became so furious she walloped him with her cane for letting the mice get in. Croadh knew that Comgall had charmed the mice into doing this to punish him, so he went to his root cellar and brought up bags of potatoes and carrots and leeks and turnips and set three copper pots boiling with a thick potato soup for all his hungry people.

We do not know whether he was *really* sorry for not loving his neighbor, or whether he was afraid the mice might come back and get the rest of his food if he didn't share it. Only God knows that. However, Comgall and his friends had a lovely supper of soup and crusty oat bread, made from the grain which the mice had shared with him.

David of Wales

Once upon a time there was a boy named Dewi, who was the son of Sant of Ceredigion and of Non, the granddaughter of Brychan of Brecknock. He went to school at Henfynyw in Cardigan, and when he grew up, he became a priest and built a monastery in Llangfelach and churches in Colfan and Glascwm and Gwent. When he was a bishop, he lived in Mynyw, and after he died, the story of his life was written by the scholar, Rhygyfarch.

Now, if you can say all *that* without tripping over your tongue, you must be a Welshman, and you must know that Dewi, or David, is the patron saint of Wales.

Wales is a country which we know for the beauty of its song and hills, and its poets and singers. But the Wales in which David was born in the sixth century was a wild, remote and somewhat forbidding land whose natives were still new to the idea of being Christians.

David was baptized in the new religion because his parents were Christians. He never wavered or was tempted away from it. And even as a child he knew that he would be a priest so he could spread the good news of Christ's gospel throughout Wales. David was direct as an arrow; he knew what he wanted and he sprung straight ahead to his goal.

He loved being outdoors (he was strong and sharp and light on his feet; if they played soccer in those days, he would have been the goalie). Most of all, David loved running. He ran along the shore, in and out of the jutting boulders, slipping on seaweed, dodging the waves, and thrilling to the feel of being one with the sand and sky and wind and God.

Then he would run along the roads which the Roman legions had built, and he would wish they were still there, working and building and sharing their knowledge with him. But after 500 years of bringing their laws and trade and new ideas to England, the Romans had gone back to their home in Italy. Now England and Wales could be invaded by the people called "barbarians," who came from all sides. These barbarians did not believe in Christ or his way of life, and rather than discuss their differences sensibly, they simply killed all Christians who got in their path.

The paths of these barbarians were the same roads David had run upon so lightly when he was a boy, and which he now walked, only a bit slower, as a priest. His job, he felt, was to travel about to preach and encourage the Christians to stand firm and keep the faith. Once, when David was speaking to a small bunch of farmers mowing hay in a meadow, a white dove, sparkling in the sunshine, flew down and settled on his shoulder.

At the same time, the molehill upon which he was standing began to grow and rise higher and higher, until it had become a small mountain.

David was surprised naturally, but he kept on speaking because he thought what he had to say was more important than a molehill turning into a mountain. It is said that his voice could be heard for miles, clear as a trumpet calling sleepers to awake.

David would do anything to prove his trust in God. Once, when his people were frightened of the Saxons who were preparing to attack, clanging their heavy shields and flying their colors on long, fierce spears, David spoke firmly.

"Do not fear them, my brothers, for we fight for the Lord, and He is with us! What do you fear? Their spears? Look beyond them, look—" And he bent down, pulled a leek (a strong-minded member of the onion family) from the earth by his feet and stuck it lightly in his wool cap.

"Look to this leek! It is as mighty as a sword in God's hands—and so are we who are in God's hands!" And a great courage came over the Welsh people. They cheered and gave small joyful hoots as they took to the patch of woods around them, looking for leeks to tuck into their own caps.

Then David and his army of farmers and blacksmiths and cheesemakers and scholars ran to meet the thundering, grunting band of savage warriors. The Saxons were taken aback by this strange sight. They turned around, pointed their spears towards the ground, and fled back into their own country, or at least out of sight of these strange-acting people with the peculiar smell. To this day, the little leek is special to a Welshman. And the true Welshman, no matter where he or she lives, wears a leek in his or her hat on March 1, the feast of St. David.

David traveled for ten more years, stopping here and there to build a church or monastery. At one town, he found the water so bad, he wondered how the people lived. They couldn't use it for drinking or cooking or bathing and they were in a terrible state—thirsty, hungry and quite dirty. David blessed the water and it became icy cool and pure at the sound of his voice. Then he blessed the place where people bathed, and the water bubbled up hot and sudsy, just right for a bath. And that is how the town of Bath, England, got its name.

One night an angel visited David in his sleep and told him that he was to build the greatest of his monasteries and it was to be at Mynyw in Wales. So back David went to begin a very simple life, quite different from that of a traveler and a preacher. He and his monks worked the land. They hoed and raked and planted and dug, growing all the vegetables they would eat. They baked a hard bread from barley and oats and drank only water. They would kill no animal nor eat any meat or fish.

That kind of life must have been good for David, for it is said that he lived to be one hundred and forty-seven years old. The night David died, St. Kentigern in Llanelwy saw his soul being carried up to heaven by four angels, who, no doubt, were wearing a garland of leeks in their hair.

Dorothy

Once upon a time in the country called Cappadocia, there lived a young girl named Dorothy who was as good as she was beautiful. Even then in the third century, this was unusual. Usually when girls are pretty, they spend their days worrying if their hair is curly enough, if the stars in their eyes sparkle, if their feet are too big, or if they smell as nice as cinnamon. That doesn't leave much time for thinking about being good. But Dorothy was unusual. She was beautiful without thinking about it, and she was good because she thought about that a great deal.

Dorothy was also a Christian, which in those days took courage. Christians lived in hiding, and they gathered in underground places called catacombs. If they were caught, they were killed as soon as possible. Dorothy's parents died this way, so she came to depend on the Lord to give her food and a place to sleep, and he always did. As Dorothy grew older, she became more beautiful and word of the special maiden reached the ears of the governor, whose name was Sapricius.

When she was brought before him, Sapricius thought, "What a lovely girl! What a shame to kill her just because she is a Christian. She is too young to know how foolish she is. Suppose I give her a chance to mend her ways...." Aloud he said, "Dorothy, if you give up this silliness of being a Christian, I will let you live. And besides that, I will marry you!" He felt very generous and pleased with himself. How could she refuse?

"Oh, I'm sorry, governor," she said. "It's very kind of you, but that just would not do. I could not live with a tongue that told lies and a heart heavy with sorrow that I had done so. I will have only the Lord for my spouse, no other. But please don't take it personally."

While she was speaking to Sapricius, a young lawyer who was very bright and who often came to the court to observe the foolish Christians being sentenced to their death, listened to her and shook his head. What a waste, such a pretty young girl!

The lawyer whose name was Theophilus tried his logic with her. "Dorothy, how can you bear to give up all the beautiful things of this world? The moon rippling on the water at night, olive trees in bloom, red pomegranates for dessert. . . ."

She smiled back at Theophilus. "Don't you think I shall have all that and more in paradise when I am with my Lord? The only reason I am *here* is to get *there*."

"Enough of this," said Sapricius, a bit annoyed at being turned down. Besides, he had twenty-seven more Christians to sentence before supper. "You want to die as a Christian?"

"Yes!" Dorothy replied.

"You want to be in paradise?"

"Oh, yes!"

"Very well, to paradise you go! Next!"

Before the soldiers led Dorothy away, Theophilus said to her with a sad smile, "Be sure to send me something from paradise, Dorothy, to show me it is as lovely as here."

"I will," Dorothy promised, feeling sorrier for Theophilus than he did for her.

As she waited in line for the executioner, an angel in the form of a little boy appeared alongside her. He carried three white roses and three apples wrapped in white linen.

"Well, imagine that!" said Dorothy, who hadn't expected to keep her promise to Theophilus so quickly. She sent the angel to find the young lawyer.

Because he was an angel, he found Theophilus in no time, at his home, feasting and drinking blackberry wine and laughing loudly with his friends. He was telling everyone he was expecting a gift from heaven and they were all laughing at the thought. "Those Christians," he laughed, "you have to admire them for their way with a joke!"

Then suddenly the room fell silent as the angel stepped up to Theophilus. His friends fell back, blinded by the rays of light surrounding the angel-child who handed Theophilus the flowers and fruit wrapped in linen.

"Dorothy sends you these from paradise," he said and immediately vanished.

Theophilus knew that Dorothy's gifts were not of this world, not only because they were brought by an angel, but also because it was February and every growing thing was asleep under the frozen earth.

The next day Theophilus appeared in court again, but this time he stood in the line of Christians awaiting sentence.

"What is this, Theophilus, you are having fun with me?" Sapricius asked.

"No, my friend, I come before you because I now believe in Dorothy's Christ and I want to join her in paradise."

And so he did.

Edward the Confessor

Once upon a time when England was very young, there was a king called Ethelred the Unready. That is not a name to be proud of, but Ethelred deserved it. He was never prepared for an emergency, as you might expect a king to be, and it was a real emergency when the Danes from the northern country overran and conquered England.

Ethelred got flustered as usual but finally recovered his wits enough to send his two sons, or "ethelings," to France for safety. They spent many years in exile waiting for a time when it would be safe for them to come home. In the meantime, Ethelred died, their mother married the Danish King Canute and left England. After all the Danes had died or been murdered, England became England again, and one of the sons, Edward, was called back to rule the country.

There could not have been a better king. Edward was ready, as Ethelred had not been, to help his country. When Edward came back, the land was poor, the people sad, and money very low. The wars had left England in a bad way. Slowly, by showing his concern for the people, Edward began to change and improve their lives. The people had nice warm homes and enough to eat, and there was a hopeful feeling in the air.

Edward was determined to be a father to his people and show how good a Christian king could be. He even looked like a father, with snow white hair and rosy cheeks. He walked among his people, fished and hunted with them.

Edward is said to have had the power of healing in his hands and sick people were cured by his touch. One day a cripple named Michael told him that St. Peter had promised to cure him if the king of England would carry him on his back to the church. Edward said, "Of course, hop up and put your arms around my neck," and Michael did.

When they reached the altar, Michael got down and slowly, very carefully, he took a step. Then another and another, and finally he began to skip down the aisle. The king and the cripple, who was no longer lame, hugged each other and Edward cheered in his heart, "Thank you, Lord!"

Edward believed that everyone was equal in God's eyes and he treated whomever he met as if he or she were Christ. When it came time to marry, Edward went out to the moors and asked a shepherd for his daughter's hand, after first asking her if she would be willing to marry him. She accepted with delight, for she knew she would be loved and treated as if she were royally born.

Once when he was dedicating a new church (Edward liked to build churches), a beggar came up to him and asked for money to buy sandals

for his frost-chilled feet. Edward had no money but gave him instead his gold ring. The old man thanked him and said he would remember Edward's kindness always.

Many years later, some English pilgrims in Jerusalem met this same beggar who told them he was John the Evangelist. He showed them Edward's ring and asked them to take it back to the king with the message that within six months he would be taken to heaven. The pilgrims hurried home and gave the ring to the king, who recognized it and knew that he must set his kingdom on earth in order before he left it.

Edward finished building Westminster Abbey, which he had been working on for fifteen years, just in time to be the first person buried there. He left a happy country and a holy one. For years, people would gather to talk and laugh and remember the days of "Good King Edward."

Elizabeth of Portugal

Once upon a time, in the age of knights and dragons and lovely princesses who were very good, there lived one such princess named Elizabeth, whose father was the King of Aragon, in Spain. She was bright and quick and had the special gift of being stubborn. She was stubborn in the *good* sense. My dictionary says stubborn can mean "doggedly determined," and that is exactly the right way to describe Elizabeth when she set her mind to do anything.

Before she was ten, she could play the castanets and dance the fandango, tell time, recite the alphabet forwards and backwards, and jump rope a hundred and twenty-six times without missing a skip. She said with God's help there was nothing she couldn't do.

This gift of stubbornness was important but not as important as her ability to settle fights. Just by being born, she had brought her father and grandfather together as friends after many years of being enemies. In the nursery she showed the little ones how to share their jacks and coloring books, and when she gave out cookies, she made sure each one had the same amount of raisins.

At an age when most girls would be going to dancing school or sleeping over at each other's castles, Elizabeth was married to Denis, the

King of Portugal. She was twelve and he was eighteen, and neither wanted to marry the other.

Elizabeth didn't want to marry at all. She had already decided that she wanted to share her life only with God. Denis, who was a wild sort, had no feeling for this young girl his parents had selected for his bride. But in those days, your parents chose who you would marry, and that was that.

"It doesn't matter if you don't love him," the girl's mother would scold sternly, "and how do you know you don't love him? Why, you don't even know him!"

"It doesn't matter if she has big ears and a red nose and shuffles when she walks," the boy's father would twirl his moustache and frown. "She will keep your pantry well-stocked with the right wine and know how to fold the linen and give orders to the cook. And she can always wear her hair over her ears. You will be very happy!"

And sometimes, by God's grace, they were. With Denis and Elizabeth, their happiest times were when they worked in separate ways to make Portugal a prosperous country. Denis believed that if everyone worked the land and learned how to farm, they would become a healthy nation and there would always be enough to eat and enjoy.

He went out into the fields with his people and planted garbanzo beans and baled hay and became as brown and full of muscles as his subjects. At the same time, Elizabeth set up schools to train young girls how to churn butter and smoke bacon and pickle beets, and everything they ought to know to become good farmers' wives.

His people loved Denis and he enjoyed being their hero—Denis the Laborer. But inside the palace it was another story. He was selfish and greedy and would always take the last piece of cake without asking if anyone else wanted it. He was the kind of person who would pull the chair out from under you when you sat down and think it very funny.

Worst of all, he had a terrible temper. If anyone upset him by saying no when he wanted a yes, or by not laughing when he told a joke, he became as violent as a bull who had just sat on a bee. He would throw footstools and teakettles or whatever he happened to grab, and the servants at the castle became very quick to learn how to run and dodge blows.

Elizabeth, who very early in life put herself in the power of God's protection, did not run or duck. She would take a deep breath and say, "Now, Denis, is this the way for a king to behave? Would you want your subjects to see you this way?" And he would simmer down and go about the room picking up the chairs and dishes and putting them in their proper places.

When the children came, life did not get better at the castle. Constance, who was like her mother, was no problem. But Alfonso had a temper to match his father's. You can imagine that it was not very much fun to live at that palace. Every time the family had a picnic or played cards or tried to do anything together, Denis and Alfonso would find some trifle to fight over, and chicken legs and cards and Spanish olives would fly through the air as the others ran for cover.

When Elizabeth went to Mass each day, she would ask the Lord to give her the strength to get through the day ahead, whatever it might bring. No matter what it did bring, she always showed a pleasant face. "Always remember," she told Constance, "that a cheerful countenance shows a serene heart, and if you trust God, your heart *will* be serene."

When Alfonso was twenty-nine, things were so bad between him and Denis, they actually went to war against each other. They had their own armies and flags and battlefields. The queen, who loved them both because God had sent them to share her life, could not bear to think of them amidst the spears and stones and arrows and cries of hate zinging through the sky. She decided she must act. "It's about time they grew up and put an end to this foolishness. It's not only silly, it's *dangerous!*"

She found a mule in the stable (all the horses were out to battle) and made her way to the battlefield. "Pardon me," she excused herself politely to a bunch of soldiers who were in her way, and she rode right smack down the middle of the field just as Denis and Alfonso were about to charge each other.

Nobody moved when they saw her. The soldiers were frozen with surprise. Elizabeth sat quietly and without a word looked from her husband to her son. Denis' and Alfonso's first thoughts were to protect Elizabeth and they came to her side quickly. She put her arms around both of them and asked them, without scolding, if for God's sake and hers they would make peace with each other and come home. Why did they waste all this precious energy in trying to kill each other and these good men when they could put it to use for Portugal?

They began to weep. Never once, in all their years of fighting, had they thought of how she had quietly listened and suffered. Alfonso knelt and asked his father's forgiveness and kissed his hand. Denis blessed his son and forgave him, and they all went home, Elizabeth leading the way on her mule. From that time on, she was known as Elizabeth the Peacemaker, and she was loved as much as Denis by her subjects.

Denis was a better husband after that, but not perfect. He still hated to see Elizabeth give away the royal food and money to the poor, and, even worse, to go among the people, bringing them delicacies, such as mint jelly and strawberries. "It is not fitting a queen," he said. When she reminded him that he had worked in the fields with the men, he just said, "That was different."

But Elizabeth could not bear to see anyone go hungry, especially in the cold winter months. Little children, she said, need fuel for their stomachs as well as wood for their fire. Every day, when her husband was busy playing chess, she would go out the back door of the castle with as many loaves of fresh rye bread as she could carry under her long purple robe. The people would be waiting (the word had gotten around), their hands eager for the warm crusty loaves. She would give them out quickly, bless them and tell them to go with God and not waste a minute.

One such afternoon her husband got up to stretch and looked out the window. He saw Elizabeth moving from one person to another giving them the bread. He was furious and rushed outside to catch her in the act.

"Well," he roared, "just what are you doing, Elizabeth? How dare you disobey me!" She lowered her eyes and waited to be punished. He tugged at her robe. "Open your cloak immediately!" She did, and instead of the fragrant loaves of bread, an armful of pink and scarlet roses in full bloom fell to the snowy ground. Elizabeth was as astonished as Denis but said nothing. She just smiled with delight inside that God once again had reached out and saved her.

From that time on, Elizabeth was allowed to feed and clothe the poor all she wished. Denis became a kinder person and began to appreciate the sweet holiness of his wife. And by the time he died, years later, he had almost no temper at all.

Now that she was alone, Elizabeth felt that she could serve God better if she became a member of the Third Order of St. Francis, which meant that she could live as a nun without living in a convent. She built a

small house on a sunny slope where she had a garden and beehives and a few chickens to take care of her needs. At last she had the peace she had sought for such a long time! "No more storms of passions and tempers! Now I shall get up with the sun in the morning and open my window and sing my praises to God along with the chickadee and the woodthrush. And then I shall brew my tea and sit in the rocker, with Isabella the kitten in my lap, and think, 'What shall I do for the Lord today?'"

Always, in whatever she did, she never forgot her manners. "Having good manners," she told Constance, "means more than knowing which fork to use for the oysters. It's really obeying the Second Commandment. When you think of other people first and put their good before yours, that is good manners—*and* loving your neighbor."

On the day she knew would be her last on earth, she saw a lovely Lady in a glowing white dress enter the room and stand by her bed. This will not do, she thought, and she called for a chair to be brought for her visitor. Her friends were puzzled. "There is no one here, Your Majesty."

By then, Elizabeth and the Lady were making their way up to heaven, and there was no need for the chair. But how polite of her to ask!

elix

See that little white spider scurrying across your bedroom ceiling? Watch him gracefully spinning a strand of silk so he can get down to earth, as you lie there, holding your breath for fear he will drop onto your nose! See him lower himself closer and closer, as you raise your hand to snuff out his life . . . Wait! Let him go about his life as you do yours, and listen to the tale of Fidelis.

Once upon a time there lived a pope named Felix. He lived at a time when it was a crime against the country to be a Christian. The followers of Christ spent their days running from one hiding place to another, trying to outwit the Roman police. There were no cars or trains or helicopters to whisk them off to a safe country. So they lived with their leader, Felix, bravely facing the fact that being caught meant certain death. If they had to die for our Lord, very well, they would. But if by prayer and grace they lived, then they might continue to tell others God's good news.

The Roman soldiers grew angrier and more threatening, and they declared that they were going to bring Felix before the Emperor. Felix was not a coward but he thought that a leader in hiding would be better than no leader at all, so he took off his royal robes and tall hat and put on the ragged brown robe of a pilgrim. He grabbed a gnarled thorn stick, hunched over and shuffled down the street.

Soon he met a bunch of rowdy soldiers. They stood in front of Felix so he could not walk and said roughly, "Hey, old man! Since you are coming from the direction of the Pope's house, have you seen him, that Christian, Felix? We have some questions to ask him." And they laughed harshly.

"No," Felix said, blowing his nose so his voice was muffled. "I have not met him," he answered truthfully. They let him go and hurried off. Felix hurried too—in the other direction. He knew they would be on to his trick soon and he had better travel quickly. Where, he did not know.

He stopped to catch his breath by a cracked wall with a hole in it. This would be as good a place as any to hide, Felix thought. So he squeezed his body through the hole, knowing that he could still be seen, but where else could he go?

He prayed, "Dear Lord, if you want me to stay in this world to lead your Christians, please get me out of this mess! What am I to do?" At that moment, a small white spider ran across the stone wall, stopped at the hole, and quickly, gracefully, began to spin a web of glossy silk over it. She spun fast, over and over in a crisscross of lines until the hole was woven from view.

Felix heard the clanking of the soldiers' shields as they returned and the scuffling of their feet on the road. He held his breath as the soldiers stopped. He heard the leader say, "He's not here, that's for sure. This spider's web hasn't been touched for days. Now where could that old man have gone? Let's get moving!" And Felix breathed again.

The Roman soldiers never did catch him, thanks to his faithful friend, the spider. Felix named the spider Fidelis, the "faithful one," because of his loyal devotion. Fidelis stayed with the Pope until Felix found another hiding place, an old dried-up well nearby. One day, when he was crouched down in the well, his stomach growling and carrying on with hunger, Felix heard his name whispered.

He knew the voice to be that of a Christian lady who had been searching for him. She had brought a loaf of rye bread and never did food taste so good. She brought food to the Pope this way for many months, until he was once more able to come out and live in the open again.

Felix never forgot his friend Fidelis, and forever after let spiders roam about his home at will. He especially liked the lovely designs they spun in the corners of windows, which caught the sunlight at dawn. Felix said they reminded him of God's light caught in a willing heart.

Genevieve

Once upon a time, there lived a young shepherdess named Genevieve who became the patron saint of the city of Paris. Genevieve was born in the village of Nanterre, not far from Paris, and soon as she was able to toddle along with him, she began to help her father tend sheep.

One day, when Genevieve was about seven years old, there was much excitement in the village. A well-loved bishop named Germain was to pass through the town on his way to Britain, where he had been sent by the Pope to settle disagreements among the Christians.

Everyone gathered in the church for his blessing. Genevieve sat huddled between her mother and father, wondering what all the hushed whispering was about, but she didn't really care. She loved being in church and feeling close to God, and that was enough for her.

The bishop walked down the aisle, smiling and giving his blessing right and left. When he came to Genevieve, he stopped and looked deeply into her eyes, and she looked back, just as intently. It must have been instant affection between the two holy souls.

"My child," he said to her, "you wish to give your whole life to Christ, do you not?"

Genevieve wondered how he knew and nodded *Yes.*

"Well," he put his hand on her head, "you shall, from this moment on." He reached into his pocket and brought forth a gold medal with a cross on it hanging from a golden chain. He put it carefully around her neck and said, "This cross is to remind you that you belong to God and will serve Him always."

Germain continued on his journey to Britain, and Genevieve went back to minding the sheep. Every Sunday she pleaded to be taken to Mass, and then she began asking to go during the week. Her mother was not happy with all this begging. There was work to be done and she couldn't have the girl flying off in the midst of milking or churning or cleaning the stables.

The mother said *No*. Genevieve kept begging, until finally her mother slapped her hard and said, "There, now do you know I mean *No* when I say *No?*"

At that moment, her mother lost her sight. She couldn't see the egg she had been scrambling or the breeze rippling the curtain. She was completely blind.

"Oh, what have I done," she sobbed, "I didn't mean to hurt her, God, I'm so sorry. Please give me back my sight!"

But even though she prayed and Genevieve prayed, she could see nothing. It took two years of Genevieve's praying before God answered

Yes. Genevieve went to their well one morning as usual, drew a pot of water, made the sign of the cross over it, and brought it to her mother to wash her face.

As soon as the woman touched it to her eyes, a blur of colors and shapes and lovely familiar things danced before her. She saw a blue pitcher filled with cream and a vase of narcissus and the happy face of Genevieve, sharp and clear, as if she had never been blind. She was so happy, she vowed never again to keep her daughter from going to church.

Eight years later Bishop Germain returned from Britain and stopped at Nanterre to see the little girl he could not forget. The little girl was now fifteen and overjoyed to see him. She told him that she wished to become a nun, and he heard her vows that she would spend her life for Christ right then and there.

Then her parents died, and Genevieve went to live with her god-mother in Paris. Godparents are so important, because if your parents go to Heaven before you grow up, it's such a comfort to know you have god-parents to help you over the bumps of growing up.

In Paris, Genevieve lived as a nun, but in her own home. She found that she had a gift of healing in her hands, especially when she used them for massage. All her love and compassion flowed through her fingers into aching backs and stiff necks and twisted ankles. She carried a small bottle of oil in her pocket to use when she massaged, and when she had run out of oil and had no way to fill it, she asked God to please do something about it.

And He did. When she uncorked the bottle, a lovely fragrance popped out. It made people smile and feel good just to smell it. As long as she lived, the bottle was never empty. What a marvellous father God is, thought Genevieve, to take care of such a tiny request!

She healed people's souls too, by spending the night kneeling in prayer for them. The devil didn't like the idea of this young woman spreading so much goodness around, especially in a city where he was used to stirring up lots of trouble.

He would come into her room as she prayed and blow out her candle. Over and over she would light it, and then he would gleefully snuff it out. She thought, "Very well, let him do his tricks. I shall ignore him."

She prayed in the moonlight coming through the window at just the right slant to bathe her in light. Then he would chase a cloud across the moon.

Finally Genevieve said, "Enough of this." And she set her mind to praying him back to his own dark world. The candle relit itself, and try as the devil might, he could not make it go out. She laughed and laughed, and the devil made a mean face and slunk out of the room.

He never bothered her again, for if there is anything the devil hates, it is to be made fun of. He has absolutely no sense of humor, when the joke's on him.

When Genevieve was twenty-nine, she worked a miracle which made her forever loved by the people of Paris. The city was on the verge of being attacked by a band of barbarians led by Attila the Hun, also known as the Scourge of God. He was as mean as his name. He rode a coal-black horse to match his black bush of a beard and fierce eyebrows that bristled every which way.

He was known to be a cruel and savage enemy, so the people of Paris were in a panic getting ready to leave and hide out in the country-side. Genevieve tried to change their minds. "Don't run away, this is *our* home. Paris needs us! Let us go to the church where we will pray until the Hun turns away from our beautiful city!"

The generals called her silly and some said she was a spy for Attila. Others just shook their heads and said she wasn't quite right in hers. How could praying change the mind of the ruthless Attila? Just saying his name caused shivers of fear to run up and down their spines.

But Genevieve and her friends paid no heed and kept praying to Our Lord to save their city. They even thanked Him ahead of time for doing so.

And of course, Attila did change his mind. We don't know why. Maybe he was tired and decided to go south instead of east. Maybe he had a bad headache from all the noise or swollen ankles or a rash. Only God knows why he didn't attack Paris.

Genevieve lived until she was ninety years old, and when she died, she was buried in the Church of Saints Peter and Paul in the heart of Paris. Even though she was gone, her miracles continued. All people had to do was ask, and she answered.

Once a terrible plague called the "Burning Fire" spread through Paris. It had already claimed fourteen thousand lives before desperate mothers began praying to Genevieve to save their children. From that moment, not one person caught the disease, and those who had been sick, recovered. The Pope declared this day a time for rejoicing and set aside every November 26 as a day for the people to celebrate their love for Genevieve.

So if some night when you feel very hot and very cold at the same time, and your bones ache, and when you lie down, there is someone playing a kettle drum in your head, call on Genevieve.

She is the saint who will dissolve fevers and chase away plagues. She will probably rub your forehead gently with her sweet oil and tell you to close your eyes, and think of all the wonderful things you will do when you are better.

$\mathcal{H}$ubert

Once upon a time in the court of Pepin, king of Belgium, there lived a young count named Hubert. Hubert was a charming, well-liked fellow who loved the good things of life—wine, food and friends, dancing, hunting and feasting. Most of all, the young count loved his beautiful wife, Floriban. He had everything that could please a man and the joyful disposition to enjoy it.

One morning Hubert woke and exclaimed, "Ah, look at this gorgeous day! I tell you to live is the most wonderful thing in the world, and the day is absolutely perfect for hunting!"

"But Hubert, dear, are you sure you must go hunting today?" Floriban asked in her gentle way.

"Of course, my darling, there couldn't be a better day. It shouldn't go to waste," Hubert answered.

"Today is Good Friday," she reminded him.

Hubert thought a moment and then shrugged his shoulders. "I'm sure the deer don't know that." He loved God but he was sure God understood about hunting.

So he kissed his wife good-bye and told her to say a prayer for him.

Then he gathered his friends and with high excitement and shouts they were off, thundering through the Ardennes Forest.

They rode into the thickest part, past huts of poor thin peasants, and split off, each going a different direction. Hubert soon knew that he had never been in this part of the forest before. He was alone and every sound he made echoed. Hubert's horse came to a stop and there in a clearing stood the largest stag Hubert had ever seen. The animal turned its head and stared at Hubert with deep, wounded dignity.

Hubert was blinded by a shaft of light which shone in the form of a cross between the stag's antlers, and on the cross hung the body of Christ. A voice said, "Hubert, turn to the Lord." The horse bowed its head and Hubert dismounted and knelt in the grass.

"What would you have me do?" he asked.

The voice said, "Go to Lambert, he will tell you."

Then the stag disappeared. Hubert stood up and rubbed his eyes. This was too real to have been a dream. He climbed slowly back onto his horse and turned it towards home. He did not feel like hunting anymore. Lambert was the bishop and Hubert knew he must go to see him. But he was fearful of what Lambert might tell him he must do. He was so happy with Floriban, he could not bear to part from her.

"Later, Lord, not yet, please!" he prayed in his heart and tried to

forget the voice in the forest. For three years he and Floriban lived happily in their love. Then a son was born to them and Floriban died. Hubert's heart was broken and he heard again the voice saying, "Go to Lambert."

So he took his son, Floribert, and went to the bishop. When he told his tale to the bishop, that wise man nodded and said he had been waiting for him. Lambert said that Hubert must now return to the forest at Ardennes, no longer as a hunter but as a hermit for the next ten years, and then he should go to Rome as a pilgrim. Floribert stayed with Lambert, and he grew up a good and lively child.

For ten years, Hubert lived as poorly as the peasants he used to ride past when hunting. Now he protected the deer instead of stalking them. Never again would he shoot any animal.

He went to Rome as he was supposed to do and there he was made a bishop to take Lambert's place. So Hubert left his beloved forest to tend the city of Tongern. This was where he was needed and Hubert did his best with his new work. After many years building churches and walls, making laws and appointing good men to serve the people, Hubert returned to the forest and its people, and Floribert, his great joy, accompanied him.

When Hubert died, the people of the forest buried him in the clearing on the spot where the stag had faced him and said, "Hubert, turn to the Lord!"

Feastdays

Alice . . . . December 16

Ambrose . . . . December 7

Anne . . . . July 26

Barbara . . . . December 4

Benedict of San Fradello . . . . April 4

Christopher . . . . July 25

Clement . . . . November 23

Comgall . . . . May 10

David of Wales . . . . March 1

Dorothy . . . . February 6

Edward the Confessor . . . . October 13

Elizabeth of Portugal . . . . July 4

Felix . . . . May 30th

Genevieve . . . . January 3

Hubert . . . . November 3

Ethel Pochocki

Ethel Pochocki has described herself as "an ordinary person" who happens to "make soup and raise kids and write stories." Both kitchencraft and the experience of raising children—eight of them, now grown up—have contributed to a whimsical, down-to-earth and understanding touch that cause her stories to make ready friends. Ethel Pochocki writes books, tales and articles for both children and adults. Though born in Bayonne, New Jersey, she has lived for many years in Maine, currently in the little town of Brooks. Here she continues to concoct adventures with the ordinary but vivid ingredients of life—"books, cats, music, frogs, hollyhocks." Out of her lifelong insight into the way facts mix with fancy and heaven mingles with earth, comes *Once Upon a Time Saints*.

Tom Matt

Tom Matt, the son of a sculptor and a painter, won awards in highschool for his own achievements in art and entered Boston University's School of Fine Arts. Soon, however, he joined the Missionary Fathers of Charity. Over a seven and a half year period, he lived and studied with them in Brooklyn, Tijuana, and Rome, serving the poorest of the poor. During the last two years he has returned to the intensive study of art at the Lyme Academy in Connecticut and now at the School of Visual Arts in New York, where his special interest is graphic design. *Once Upon a Time Saints* is his first illustrated book.